THREE WINTER TALES

DEREK ALLAN

DEDICATION

To all the people in my life who have given me love, hope, and magic.

CONTENTS

ACKNOWLEDGMENTS

All these magical moments they never leave, through the
good and the bad I'll always believe.

THE PAPERBOY

Once again it was time for the first Autumn walk of the year.

Whether in rain, shine or wind (usually all three) it didn't matter, it must be done. It had always been done and always would be.

Walking through the seasons fills you with all you need to get you through the year. We think differently through every season until every month and every thought makes sense or can be forgotten and ignored.

This Autumn time for Carl meant he had just turned 11. He had been 11 for well over one week now and this meant that the countdown to Christmas was here.

His walk started off with his dad and stories of the past, his own and theirs together. Stories of what they will do to make this year even better than the last. Learning to better yourself and the lives of others is the reason people arrive in this world.

The logs were on the fire waiting to be lit once they got back home. It was always nice to walk home in the cold knowing that it was going to be so warm inside. It made him feel cozy and loved. The hot chocolate and the marshmallows added to the warmth and the feeling of being loved. Autumn was a wonderful month to be in and perfect for preparing for the Winter.

Carl loved to fall behind so that he could run and catch up to his dad. It was a great feeling as he got closer because that smile that he would never forget would turn to face him and stay with him for the whole season. It was the smile that would light up the beginning of Autumn. The steady lead up to Christmas.

Dad loved it when Carl fell behind so that he would have to catch him up. He would hear the hurried footsteps as his little boy neared and hear his breathing. He would turn to see his magical smile as he arrived back by his side and their smiles would join and last forever. This was the beginning of a new season. It was always an exciting time. The cold waking you up for the months ahead.

Carl had long shoulder length blonde hair, like his dads but half the length. Dad looked just as strong as he actually was, all muscle from his life of helping out on the farms from boy to man.

Once back at the cottage the milk would be in the pan and heated through for the hot chocolate the logs in the living room fireplace would be lit. It was Autumn and Dad would start a book and read it every day until it was read. This year it was "The Water Babies". They spent a lot of time in the kitchen. It was a place to relax without feeling too tired.

Their Sunday morning walk was their favourite walk of the week. Down the path to the road leading into the village. Only a few minutes wander but on a Sunday, it wasn't about distance it was more about the adventure. Over the fence and down by the stream. So many stickleback fish had been caught here in the past and would be again. Put into jars and inspected before being released.

The stream was a great sound, heard mostly in the Autumn and Winter as they would pause for a listen as they passed.

This walk always had them thinking about the walk that David Essex took in "A Winter's Tale". They would sing it as they neared the pond. Carl loved the life in the pond It froze over in the Winter and it seemed to sleep away until the warmth of the sun could once again be felt. Everything in the pond that once acted like it wanted to be seen, was hiding, leaving the pond still and in silence. There is something about a pond that makes you feel happy and alive that little bit more. Maybe it is because of the endless life in that simple little pond, a pond of life.

They were inside the post office by 8 AM and looking for a new model airfix plane to build for when the rain next fell. They picked up a TV guide and a mix up of sweets. Although Carl had seen the shop every week for his whole life, he always liked to have a look around at all the things the old paper shop sold.

"Good morning Ken." said Carl. "Any news in?"

"Just what is in the paper." replied Ken smiling, knowing what the response would be.

"That's not news." Carl said and smiled up at his dad. Happy to be echoing the words he had heard him say many times before. They never bought the newspaper. There was nothing in there for them, here in the village, here in their own lives.

"Oh, Carl...I meant to say" said Ken pointing at a note pinned to the wall" what about that new job up there? You should take it you know! You don't get too many jobs offers around here. You are next in line now that Daniel has packed up and left the village with his family."

4

Carl walked over to the notice board where his dad was standing. They stared at it for a while and then they looked at each other.

"Would you like to do it?" Dad questioned "Taking the news to everyone,

"Is this a good job?" asked Carl.

"The people here like the news otherwise the Newspapers wouldn't be here." Dad replied.

"Well, if you think it is a good idea then I think it is too." Carl was beginning to get excited

"I think it will do you good." said dad "You can save up some pennies for some of your very own new things."

Pleased with this idea Carl happily announced to Ken "Tell me what to do and I'll take it."

"Oh, this is wonderful news" Ken Said. "A new paperboy in the village. This is indeed the top news of the week! Daniel will be on his last round today and you can take over straight away. This means I don't have to fill in, which is actually a good thing as I don't have a bike and it would have taken me a long time" Ken laughed a little laugh.

The piece of paper that Ken had handed to Carl had a hand drawn map on it and numbers on the square drawn houses. These were the houses that liked the newspapers delivered to their homes. There were not too many but enough to earn a wage and save up for something new. Carl and his dad walked the route so that Carl knew where to go when it was time.

The week was an exciting one as they both made plans and talked about some of the past jobs that his father had done. Since Carl had arrived, he was mostly a "part time" this and a "part time" that, as by choice, he was a full time, Dad. This to him was the best job in the world, it took up all of his time but in a good way, in a great way. There is no slowing life down or turning back time so you have to learn from everyone and everything around you to choose the best life that you can live.

On his bike and on his own Carl set off with the bag of paper printed with news from around the world from the paper shop. The feeling was too much to take. He felt electric, like he could fly on his bike. He loved doing little jobs for his dad and taking anything to anyone always made him happy. This feeling was even better!

The farm was the first house to receive a paper from Carl. Ted came out to meet him at the door. Ted was old enough to retire but "a farmer's work is never done". He nodded his cap wearing head, his grey hair escaping out of the back. He cared little for his appearance and more about getting through each day.

"Good morning," Ted said "A new paper lad and right on time too! You have a great life ahead of you and you have started out well. Being on time is so important and I for one am pleased that you have arrived when I hoped you would arrive. "He smiled and Carl did too as he ran up to hand over the paper. He was filled with pride.

The baker was next, even though he no longer worked in a shop he still continued to do what he did best. You could tell from looking at him that he was very happy to eat everything he baked and that he baked often.

"Hello Tom. I have your paper." said Carl excitedly.

"Thank you, would you like to take a cake with you?" Tom grinned. His hair still had a little red in it and was sticking up showing off his very bess morning look.

"Oh, yes please. And one for my dad?"

"Don't worry, I would never leave your dad out." Tom popped into his house. The cakes were boxed already and he handed them over to Carl. Carl wasn't tempted to eat one. He was contributing to the family tea time and this made him happy right through. He wanted to see the face of his dad when he handed over the surprise.

Brian was a bus driver when he was younger. He still did occasional private runs for people, but he was very rarely needed these days. He was at the door smoking a pipe when Carl arrived at his cottage. Long grey hair in a ponytail.

"Good morning Carl. and a lovely Autumn morning it is." Brian was good with people having been a bus driver. He had met people of all kinds. Nice people, not so nice people, stressed people, happy people, sad people, truthful people, you get it, I am sure.

"Here you go. I hope that adds to your morning." Carl handed over the paper.

"Yes, it's sure to cheer me up. Reading about strangers doing strange things." Brian laughed and turned the paper to the sports news at the back.

Bill just stayed at the window. He nodded to Carl as he neared the door. Carl pushed the paper through the letter box and looked around at the amazing garden. There was a small lawn surrounded by so many different lighthouses. It looked incredible. Bill was a soldier when he was younger but these days he liked to stay out of the way from people and spend time with the tv and in the garden. This way he had the best of both of the worlds he enjoyed.

Carl looked up at the window once he realised that he had stared around the lighthouse garden for too long and smiled. Bill nodded, almost smiled and then disappeared from view. He would come and meet Carl in time, but not today.

Shane was the local gardener. He had travelled many miles in his life to do what he does best and better than most. Another one of those jobs that you can never retire from. His garden was never this good when he worked his usual 50 hours a week. Now that he had more time it was the greatest garden in any village. The greatest garden in any village in all the land.

"Leave it at the doorstep, Carl."

"I have a new job, Shane."

"I can see that."

"I love it."

"I can see that too." Shane said as he carried on with his gardening.

Sue stood at the door drinking tea and was very happy to

see a very happy boy being very happy in his new job and with his life in general. Smiling as he arrived as if he was her own son. Her hair was in a bun and was bright white.

"Good morning. Are you enjoying your new job?"

"Ah, I love it, Sue. I think it is the best job a lad like me could have"

"You will be good at everything you do Carl because you live life with a smile for company."

"I hope I can do it forever like my dad does."

"A smile like yours never fades and your dad will make sure of this."

Barnes was a retired fisherman. He had a garden filled with boats, each one with flowers and plants growing inside. Shane had helped with the garden. A little part time work turned the Barnes' Garden into a masterpiece. One of the boats was good enough and big enough to live in but there was no one around the village needing to live in a boat in his garden.

"Hello to you Carl."

"I have your paper."

"I can see that. Has it been a good first day?"

"I just love it Barnes, so fresh out here."

"It will get a lot colder over the Winter but I doubt that it will bother you."

Carl handed over the paper and was on his bike again. "Every season has its warmth." he shouted as he cycled away.

Ken was standing with a 50p mix up of sweets for Carl when he returned to the shop. Carl couldn't wait to tell Ken how it all went.

"Here is a bonus for you. Very well done on your first day and not one complaint." Ken joked.

Carl stepped inside. "Have people ever complained?" he asked, a little concerned. He wanted to do his job well.

"No, not here. We have a nice village. People here have enough money to never need to think about it. This means that they can enjoy life and other people with no complaints or jealousy."

"Oh, that is good. I wouldn't want to upset anybody."

"You are a villager for life Carl, you will always feel happy and safe here."

The houses with no one at the door or in the garden got their papers through the letterbox.

These are the rules. Don't disturb people if they are not around. They aren't around because they are usually doing something they like to do otherwise they wouldn't be doing it.

The final house was on the way out of the village and although it was an entire field away this was the neighbour of Carl and his dad.

Elaine didn't look happy. She smiled a little smile but it didn't last and it was gone before Carl even handed over the paper.

"Good morning, Elaine. Are you ok?"

"I have never been ok and there is no time left to do better. She said sadly, "Thank you for the paper and thank you for asking how I am."

"Is something wrong?" Carl felt pains running through him. He had no experience of sadness but he imagined that this looked like the look of sadness.

"Choices my dear boy, it is all about choices. They are mostly made for you without your knowledge. I suppose it is better that way as you have someone else to blame"

Carl didn't speak. He just looked down at the floor.

"Just be yourself dear boy" she said "Do you know, people will always tell you to be yourself, then when you are, they dislike you as you remind them that they were never themselves at all"

He still didn't know what to say and all he could think of was "I'll see you next Sunday."

"If I am still here." Elaine said.

Carl suddenly felt the Autumn cold as he ran for his bike and back home to share the morning with his dad.

They ate porridge with honey and went for a walk to find fallen branches for the fire and talk about his new job and the villagers.

October was a great month for them. A lot of happiness and a lot of fun mixing up the minutes to make some fantastic hours. Carl played his favourite tape every day. It was a mix of music called "Now Music 9". He took it to the car every time they went for a drive and played it in the house when the radio was not playing out the songs of its choice.

Their backroom had a tape player and a dartboard in it. He was not very good at darts but he didn't know it. He would spend time throwing for the bullseye and taking in the wonderful smell of Blackberry Jam being made in the room next door.

Picking Blackberries was a lot about the stings and scratches but it was all worth it every time. He loved the Blackberry Spider that was always there too. At every thorny bush with a giant web big enough to catch any fallen berries. He thought maybe it was the same spider just following them around.

Jackie Wilson was singing "Reet Petite" and Mental as Anything were singing "Live It Up" as Carl threw and collected the darts over and over again. He never got tired of this. He had no idea that as from Christmas day this games room would have something new added to it and he would be playing with Pacman, Q*Bert, Frogger and Space Invaders. This was for the future though and the memories and feelings would remain with him forever.

Sundays were going very well and everyone involved was happy. Joan had heard about the polite happy little paper boy and decided that she would also like a paper delivered on Sundays. The round was still only an hour in total.

Joan was once a Farmer's wife in another county but when her family grew up and her husband passed away, she moved home to spend her time as quietly as she could. Her life was very busy before now and this is what she had to show for it. A small cottage and a happy looking garden sadly no company and no knowledge about where to find any.

Carl would count his money daily wondering what he should buy with it. Shopping day would be here soon and he would spend every penny. For now, he kept on thinking. He was a thinker unlike anyone he knew but for now he just thought that he was like everyone else.

Carl got to know Ted, Tom, Brian, Ken, Bill, Shane, Sue, Elaine, Barnes and Joan very well. He met them every Sunday for a few minutes and he loved to see them all, a part of their routine, a part of his routine. They all seemed happy enough to see him and Elaine never acted the same way that she did on that first day, sad and angry.

Carl was making toast under the grill with the radio on, "Here I Go Again" by Whitesnake was playing and he sang it with all of his heart just like David Coverdale did.

The kitchen was large for a small house. Food is such a big part of our lives and takes a lot of preparing so it is best to have plenty of room if ever you get the choice. That is unless you only do takeaways, then you only need a large sofa.

There was enough room in Carl's Kitchen to dance along to Kiss as he sang "Crazy Crazy Nights".

Carl was good at keeping a watch on the toast. You have to take the toast out of the grill at just the right moment otherwise you are scraping the blackness from the bread or just eating it burned.

Toast, Jam and butter was their favourite breakfast and most of their suppers too. The jam was homemade, so they liked it even more. The cuts and stings they went through were worth it to fill up the many containers. Making enough jam to last them the Autumn and some of the winter. Carl loved to make scones too and when they made them there was always whipped cream and jam added. They were giant scones too so there was no need for seconds, just huge firsts.

Dad called on Carl, "We need to head into town soon and spend up some of that money of yours. I think Woolworths will have everything you need and we can get a pic n mix for our walk around the mid-Autumn fields. Maybe pick up a new tape."

Like Carl did every day he appreciated all things nice. He lit up and the light shone from his smile. "I have so many things in mind but I don't need a new tape yet. The one I have is fine and has all of the songs on it that I need for the moment". With his excitement brimming over Carl said "I just keep thinking of new things and old things and new things that I have never seen and it never ends. I sometimes think that just looking at all of the things in the shop is enough to keep me going."

His dad smiled and added "we can do a little extra work on Sundays if you like. I have to chop logs for the winter and I need to do enough for everyone in the village."

"You got the job?" shouted Carl.

"Yes, I did" Dad said "nice easy Sundays. The logs will be dropped off. I'll split them, you can bag them and then they will be taken away and sold. The orders are all in so I'll be chopping logs until the Winter ends in April, May or June or whenever it decides to leave." he chuckled.

"Now we both have jobs. Life just gets easier."

Stand By Me was a song they both sang along to.They always stopped what they were doing when it came on. This song made so much sense to them. Everyone should stand by someone.

The weeks moved on at a steady pace. Carl and his dad watched their favourite tv shows in the living room, played the radio and their tapes in the kitchen. They played Ludo, Chess, Card Games, Stratego, Draughts and when they had a spare day a game of Monopoly but this was a game to play only once a year if you are actually going to get to the end and enjoy it. They cooked and baked every Saturday. Carl was being taught how to do everything in life and school was teaching him the rest. He was a very happy child and this made the whole village a very happy village. Every villager could see a part of themselves in him, usually the part that they had forgotten about, but he was here to remind them.

Halloween was a nice night. A turnip lantern with a candle

inside and a black bin bag cloak. Carl was ready to walk the village asking politely at every door he knocked on "penny for the lantern." His dad took a pot for the money, it would be put into buying an extra gift for Carl. This time next year Carl would be dressed as a Ghostbuster, this would be a big year for Ghostbusters accessories. Carl liked surprises but he also knew that his dad was not rich. He never asked for anything, but he knew that he would have the best Christmas time. The buildup, the actual day and the magic of it that would last for the whole year. So, the Halloween money was put into the Christmas kitty to buy an annual bauble from the garden centre and a surprise gift.

They ended the day watching Bugs Bunny Halloween Special, Howl-Oween.

Bonfire night came and they lit a fire in the garden, old wood was collected from around the village. Broken fences, old doors and smashed up old furniture mostly. This helped tidy up the village so the people were happy to send the wood away for their fire. For food they had baked potatoes which were wrapped in foil and then thrown on the bonfire. Some salt and butter would be added once they were cooked. A box of fireworks to set off with a Catherine Wheel to end the display.

Bonfire night was a nice time in the garden. They would stay by the fire for a long time eating, drinking and talking about all that is good about life. Even one step away from the fire and they could feel the cold of mid-Autumn but the warmth from these nights would never leave,

It was only weeks away now and Carl felt it with every

breath he took. He wore a bigger coat now for the paper round. The cold was here and it would be here for a while with a few sunny days to walk over the dry frosted fields to look forward to.

Bon Jovi was "Living on a Prayer" and Europe sang out about "The Final Countdown" in the car on the way for chips, batter and a can of pop. Chippy tea night would be amazing every single time. The day had been cold so they ate the chips down by the pond in the car. So many frogs, toads and newts lived here in the Spring and the summer. But for now, they were hiding somewhere. Chips taste great wherever they are eaten but out in the cold they taste even better and they warm you up too.

The houses that let Carl put their papers in the letter boxes still never showed their faces, but the people that waited for their paper on Carl's first round were there every time. Still smiling and still with a few words to exchange with Carl.

Each one smiling and staring as they looked back deep into their lives. The part of their lives that Carl reminded them of.

"It's nearly Christmas." Carl told each one of them.

To this not one person replied, they were all hit with a feeling that Carl knew nothing about.

Their smiles changed to a smile with no feeling, just a shape on their faces. He didn't know it but Carl had moved them. These smiles were put there to hide behind. He felt that something had happened to them and he had made it happen.

It was only Joan who had replied, and Carl felt something inside that made him feel like he needed to talk to Dad about it before he got too worried.

"Christmas has been for me son" she had said in a low voice. It made Carl feel uneasy. She said almost as if she didn't mean the words to come out.

He had never mentioned Elaine and what she had said on the first day of deliveries. He had allowed himself to forget it as she had never sounded sad or cold since then.

Today though, when nobody replied with their usual friendly chat it made him feel sad too. He hoped that the next village friend would reply and fill him back up with the magic.

When Carl got home, he ate the sandwich his dad had made for him and then they went off in the car to buy the annual bauble from the Garden Centre. The garden centre was dressed up so well every year, a magical wonderland. Carl and his dad always bought one more bauble for the Christmas tree from the "Penny for the lantern" money. They always bought a fruit cake too. A lot of time had gone into preparing these cakes so the least they could do was buy one, take it home and eat it.

Every year a little more was added to the display, so the walk around took a little longer each time. Christmas cards were bought from here too. Music played around the whole centre on a radio. People looked happy and busy all around them.

Later at home they made themselves busy and Carl helped his dad to get the work done for the day, music played along to help them.

Carl learned a lot from all of the songs on his tape, he liked to listen properly to all of the words. Erasure were singing about "Sometimes" and his Question about Joan was playing on his mind.

He didn't know a good time to ask it and this added to his thoughts.

After filling a trailer with logs, they stopped for a can of Coke and a kit kat. "Do The Right Thing" was playing by Simply Red. This was the time. The song made him feel ready.

"Joan seemed sad today, Dad."

His Dad placed his can of Coke down "What makes you think that she was sad?"

"Everyone looked a little sad today. But Joan seemed sadder." Carl was clearly upset.

His Dad thought carefully about his reply. "People are only really happy for so many hours a day, week or month. The rest of the time they are busy ignoring sadness or being sad. Life is hard for other people, they are not like us, they do not have our ways. They have made their decisions in life and now they are living with them. Some people are not happy with their choices."

Carl looked thoughtful "I didn't like it, Dad. I said to them all that Christmas was coming and they didn't spark and shine and smile with me. I felt like I had pressed pause on the video."

"Ah" Dad replied, "Christmas. It is there for everyone but it is not there for everyone."

"Do some people not like Christmas?" Carl made the face of shock and sadness. He had never worn this face before, it was a new face for him to make but still, it was there for when he needed it.

"Unfortunately, like life itself, people ignore Christmas and expect it to always just be there for them. They don't realise that to have magical memories you need to make the magic yourself. You need to do this so that there are enough memories to look back on when the real thing is gone. You either have to be taught to live and be happy or learn to find happiness all on your own. This is a very very hard thing to do. Strangers get together and become friends, people bring people into the world to make up a family. So much can go wrong, so many distractions. Christmas time is a time of reflection, and it is the time when people look back on their year and on their entire lives. It is hard work being happy."

"Oh dad, that is so so sad." A tear arrived and Carl's dad caught it for him.

"Life is hard for so many people Carl. We have each other so we are happily ignoring the sad."

"Are we bad for doing this?" Carl replied, "Can we help everyone?"

"No, we are not bad. We have to love and make happy our family and our friends."

"Our village?" Carl added.

Dad smiled another smile." You make this village very happy and this makes me even happier."

"How do you know I make them happy?" Carl said.

"I can see and feel it in the village, and I hear it when they tell me. You are very special. You see what so many have never seen, and you see what many used to see, you feel it too and you share it, you share everything. You are a lighthouse, and we are candles."

"But this is the best time of the year." Carl said, still sounding confused.

"Not for everyone." Dad said in a soft voice.

"Can they all come to our house for Christmas? Can we make it special again for them?"

He loved How kind and loving Carl was "I am sorry Carl, but they wouldn't all want to come here for Christmas."

"Shall I ask them?" Carl asked hopefully.

"You can't invite one and not the rest. And the whole village couldn't all come." his dad reasoned.

"I could find out who needs us the most then?" Carl was not giving up.

"Carl, we can think of something, but we can't have

21

everyone around for dinner." Patting Carl's shoulder and picking up his can of Coke to finish the last drops he took a step forward "Ok. how about we bag up these logs. At Least we can help them all to stay warm in the winter. That is what we can do. Keep them warm through the winter."

"With love, lights, truth, happiness and logs?" Carl was smiling again like everything was fixed.

Carl was throwing for the bullseye daily and thinking more about his plans. He was still thinking up his plans whilst he was playing Ludo, Chess, draughts and Stratego but he did not want anyone to know. This was his plan, his test and his surprise. It was hard for him to understand the sadness his friends had as he did not know the pictures; he had never had his own sadness, but it was going to have to leave the village and especially at Christmas.

One of the great days of any day, week, month or year is the trip to the video shop to pick a film. Walking into the video shop could light you up inside enough to inspire you to live and be a greater person for your whole life. Film makers were magical people.

Carl knew where the new videos were, the cheaper older ones and the scary ones that he did not ever want to see. Choosing one film was never an easy choice but he knew that whichever one he chose would be perfect.

There was a second "Karate Kid" movie out now and he and his dad had loved the first one. In the newer section, the movie covers catching his eye were "Predator", "The Lost Boys", "Jaws" and "Robocop" but they all looked like they could be scary. "The Princess Bride", "Vice Versa" and "The Wind in the Willows" looked good too.

Carl spent a lifetime in movie land but after 30 minutes his dad made a suggestion, and they went home with "Planes, Trains and Automobiles".

As soon as A-HA had finished singing the last song of the trip, Carl ejected the tape and took it into the house. Baked Beans and Hot Dogs were heated in pans and hot chocolate was made up. A lot of thinking still needed doing but the movie would inspire Carl even more. There is always more good to be done.

Carl stood at the door looking at the sky like he was looking for something or someone. He was singing about the Caravan of Love. He jumped when it opened although it was, he who had knocked on it.

"Hello Carl."

"Hello Ted. I have come to talk to you if that is ok. I think we know each other well enough to be called friends. I was hoping you could share with me some of your life stories."

Ted laughed a happy laugh.

"Why are you laughing?" Carl smiled; he liked the sound of Teds Laugh

"Who in the world would find me interesting?"

"Me!" Carl said "Please tell me about when you were like me and I will be interested."

"How long do I get? Am I to be timed?" asked Ted all

excited as he walked over to his fire bin to stoke it back into life, he continued smiling as he ran through some memories. Memories he thought he would never remember again because they were losing meaning by the hour.

"Talk as long as you like, "Carl said. "I am new at this."

"How long does it take to tell a life story, and can it ever be fully told?" Ted pondered.

"Has anyone ever tried?" asked Carl "We can give it a go!"

The fire was lit up and it brought them such comfort on this cold afternoon.

"My life was set up for me," Ted started "No real plans, just that my family have all been farmers and that is what we do. At times we like it and at times we dislike it, but it has to be done. We are great at it and we teach the next generation to better us. It is not a competition, and this makes it work, we just have to win the day enough times to win the year. You must keep trying and never reach the finish line because it always moves by the time you arrive. Just keep on winning. It never ends. Being a farmer or farming. It never ends."

Ted held the familiar stare again as he looked back into a time that he usually chose to ignore.

Carl listened intently "You must be a great farmer!"

"I am. It is all I know and all I want to know. I don't wish to know the business of anyone and everyone and they should have no wish to know about mine. That is the best

way to live. I guess my life is pretty boring compared to
most lives. I farm, I always have, and I always will. Just a
little slower these days." he let out a little laugh to tell Carl
that it was not a complaint.

Carl couldn't imagine the pains of being an old man. He
had never felt a tired ache before. "Were you happy when
you were a boy?" he asked.

"I have never really known about being unhappy. I am too
busy being the person I was born to be. No comparing, no
complaining, just being little Teddy as a kid and now Ted."

"You seem happy with life," Carl said "That is good news."

"It's the only news. I am the only news I know, and I like it
to be happy. There are a lot of questions that can be
answered but we don't need the answers or believe them
otherwise we would go and find them. It is what it is."

Tom smiled, a long, look back, happy smile when Carl
asked him for stories about his childhood.

"Food is my answer" he explained "The ever-present
smells of food. The taste of food. Baking it, eating it,
selling it and making it better and better. I had a lovely,
tasty childhood."

"That is good to hear." Carl nodded, pleased with the
question, and pleased with the answer.

"I do miss those days though. My Mam and Dad trying my
freshly baked food, me trying theirs and the excitement
when someone came in the bakery and bought something
that was baked from scratch. Even better when they came

back to buy the same things again because the first time was so good."

"Did you prefer to bake some things more than others?" Carl wanted to Know

Tom slowly shook his head. "I just loved to bake and make Mam and Dad happy and proud."

"I bet you did." Carl knew what he meant.

"I know I did! Hey, would you like to take something home for you and your dad? I always need my tasters."

Tom walked into the kitchen. "Follow me."

Carl followed Tom and the smells and sight of the food melted him. He couldn't say no to taking something from this kitchen back home to his own.

"Take what you like. I always make too much anyway."

Carl took no time to choose "Two Gingerbread Christmas Bells please!"

Smiling again, Tom remembered something else. "The smells and tastes of Christmas are what I remember most of all about my childhood, especially when Winter is so close. I warm right through when I smell and taste Christmas."

Brian also liked Carl's question. It was like he had been invited back into his past rather than to sadly drift there from time to time. Sharing your past is a nice thing to do.

"I wanted to race cars," he said "This should make you

laugh! I almost made it as a racing driver but I was too reckless. I could no longer afford my dream, so I became a bus driver instead."

"This is funny. Maybe I should walk rather than take the bus from now on." Carl joked.

"You are always safe with me; I have racing driver reflexes. I love the car and I love the bus. I just love to drive and play music everywhere I go. I especially like long drives, like the ones in the back of the car with my Mam and Dad if we went on a trip when I was a kid."

Carl agreed "I like long journeys too. I usually play my favourite tape."

Brian nodded "I like a tape for the car, and I like the radio. Music is my life, well, it has always been with me. Discovering new and old bands. Buying new tapes and playing them for the first time."

Carl felt the same way "There are a lot of songs to hear."

"There are a lot of people," Brian continued "a lot of hearts to heal. We all need company. Music is my childhood and driving is my life. This time of year, I like to listen to songs I have listened to at this time of year every year. I like to try and prepare for Christmas day, for me it is a day when I look back and pick out the nice times. I try to remember the times that made me happy then. The magic of happiness is that you can bring it back to right now whenever you need it."

Shane liked the chance to be able to talk about his life

spent in gardens whilst being in his garden. It was all he knew and all that he wanted to know. Carl loved the garden and being in it felt good. A tidy place to be and so fresh and clean. He grew all of his own vegetables and kept a good mix of plants to eat and plants to look at. Every season was an ever-changing picture and Shane kept all of this magic in his very own garden. His earliest memory was helping his grandfather to dig up vegetables and have fires in the garden. Hearing about the seasons was a special memory, being told there were four different kinds of magic that all arrive at different times but work together completing the perfect year every year.

He remembered this happy warm feeling every time he lit a fire.

He imagined that this feeling came from way back in the times when we lived in the cold in caves. The first fire of life must have been a very happy warm fire, that feeling has never left and it lives on in us forever. With fire there is both magic and life.

Shane lit up a small garden fire and made up a pot of tea for his story. Tea goes with every job with or without milk and sugar.

Bill wanted to be a soldier his whole life. As a boy he played soldiers and read books and comics about soldiers. They were the brave warriors, the heroes, the fearless men that were born to save the world. Now he was retired and no longer thought or talked about being a soldier or about war. He retired earlier in life to teach children how to play cricket and football. He bought all the things that were needed to play and practice these sports and all of his love went into the sport and the children. This was what he believed in. One of the children even grew up to play for his country and he still sent letters to Bill to invite him to games and sports dinners. He never met anyone long enough to be able to have his own family, so he retired into a village away from the world. With himself was where he belonged, and this was the life he chose, and he now accepted it.

Carl loved to hear the nice in every story, but these people were so sad almost like there was not enough happy to last their lifetime.

Sue was happy on her own and had always been happy on her own. She wanted to paint and leave art everywhere she went. She knew that her art was her life and knew this was her way to spread magic in other people's lives. Her art would stay with people for all time.

If ever she felt happy or sad then she would go into the study, which was every day. She would always be working on a happy painting and a sad one. She never mixed the feelings.

Her paintings and books of her paintings had made her wealthy enough to live in this village and not need to to travel to sell her paintings. Staying home and painting was always her dream, and this dream was every day. Like all of the rest she did not like the month of December, not because this of the month was the start of Winter but because this was the only time, she thought about the people she no longer knew or never got to know. She accepted her choices, but she still did not like the feeling of what Christmas was and could be. She treated Christmas the same as the rest of the year. Her only memories of being a child at Christmas time was getting her art set and a teddy bear that she took everywhere. But Sue was not into talking about then, she felt that she belonged in the now. She painted now and she lived now, and it was up to others to look up her past and her art if they were interested but Sue was not.

Elaine was a dancer as a child. She was never going to be a big star in the world of dancing, and no one was going to ever tell her this but she was a star in her family and that was enough for her to be happy in her childhood. She went to see annual Dance shows as a child with her parents. Elaine was happy enough being in every day unnoticed. She liked to watch tv and listen to the radio. She would read book after book with two or three being delivered a week for her display. She was so inspired by these books, the thoughts, stories, magic, happiness, and sadness inside them. Tv and books lived the dreams for everyone, and Elaine liked it this way. She felt excited when watching tv or reading and afterwards she would happily turn off the tv or simply close the book. Thinking about her life before the village was not something she liked to do so after writing her memoirs some years ago she had closed that book for good.

Barnes was a fisherman and he had loved catching fish in ponds, rivers, lakes and the place where he made his living, the sea. He had made a lot of money and his family would never have had to work again, but he never had a family. He worked then he worked some more. He loved the sea as a boy and man and loved to look back on his life on the sea. He had very few friends but he had always liked it that way. Although he was friendly, he did not have time for friends.

Now that he lived in the village, he did like the idea of a friend or two. To share stories and share a drink or two would be nice but his people skills were nowhere near his fishing skills.

Carl loved the idea of being a fisherman but a lot of the stories were frightening. He thought that a normal person would never go back to sea after some of the scary times that Barnes had lived. His garden was all boats. His house was all models of boats and pictures. His life was all about boats on the sea.

Now that Carl had talked to almost everybody, he felt like he had worked out why they all looked as if they were staring back at the past, right through the now. Their faces all held the same expression because they were searching for something, Carl believed he was the key. They wanted to find themselves so he wanted to help to find them.

It was as if they wanted to go back, but they knew that even if they could, the second time around they would make the same choices. Staying here was the best place for them to stay. They all believed that they belonged in the here and now, so he wanted them to enjoy being in the place that their whole lives had led them to.

He had to work out a plan and keep thinking of it, making it better in his head before he carried it out. He also had to be careful not to be caught.

The next week he felt he was ready to speak to Joan.

He started his round a little earlier so that he could be with her longer. He woke 10 minutes earlier than usual, he never liked sleep anyway, sleep was for other people not for him and his dad. Dreams were for living.

"Hello and a great Morning Joan."

"Hello and a good Morning to you Carl."

"Can I talk to you for a little bit?" he said, feeling brave.

"What about?" she said. Carl continued "I love people of all ages and would like to hear more about your time in this life."

She seemed surprised "Because I am old you think I will be interesting?"

"We are never old," Carl said wisely, "we never live long enough."

"Are you going to speak like a wise old man to everything I say?" she said, amusement almost showing on her face.

"I just listen out for great things so that I can think and say and use them. It is best to do this or all of the great thoughts will not be passed on to the people that need them." Carl reasoned.

Joan paused then asked "What do you want me to tell you?"

"A little bit more than you would like to please?" Carl said bravely.

Joan stood and stared into a new place. A different one to

the others, somewhere deeper and more worrying. "Why would I want to tell you anything of my life?"

"You will be listening too" Carl said, so much more wisely than his years. "It is good for you to talk to yourself when someone else is there. You can hear yourself and ask yourself questions, ones that might still need answered".

Joan nodded slowly "I like to stay as happy as I can but it gets harder when you become older. Everyone and everything get older around you too. It's like you have no one to turn to. The young will never understand in time. Nothing slows down for you and eventually you can no longer keep up."

"What makes you happy?" Carl asked.

"I like to see people being happy. That really is enough for me. I like to think that they made themselves happy. I like to think that they made the right choices in their lives and that they are in love surrounded by all the right choices."

"There are a lot of happy people in the village." Carl said.

"I love the village," Joan smiled. "I know that I chose to be here and I didn't just end up here."

"Did you like Christmas when you were a little girl?"

"Oh, I sometimes forget that I was ever a little girl." She smiled a smile as if she was smiling at the little girl she once was.

"You were a happy little girl?"

"I was. And yes, I loved Christmas and everyone being there together. Back then I never felt alone at Christmas and could never imagine that I would ever be alone. The love and happiness were too strong."

December started out well with the tree up and decorated. The living room was decorated nicely and the kitchen had a few handmade decorations.

Carl and his dad collected fallen pine cones, acorns and fallen branches for the Autumn display. They dropped them around the fireplace and around the kitchen. The cold dark winter was not going to make them feel cold and afraid, they lit up the house inside. It was a magical display; it took two days to finish their work but they always had a little more to add. The radio was playing more Christmas songs from the past, Noddy shouting out "It's Christmas" and Roy Wood wishing that it could be "Christmas every day".

Memories of painting pine cones and making streamers with the music playing by the log fire would stay with them forever.

The first Monday of the month and they went Christmas shopping as usual. They always bought from small local shops to help them to stay around for longer and then to Woolworths for the main shop. Woolworths was a Christmas shopping wonderland in December.

Carl would usually get £10 from his dad and walk around the shop looking to see what to buy him each year. There was always so much and every aisle was well dressed in Christmas cheer. They could never have enough tinsel so this was added to the basket. Wrapping paper too.

This year Carl had more money to spend on his dad but this seemed to make it harder to choose, he wanted to buy his dad everything.

He continued to think about his friends in the village and wondered how best to help them and make them even happier. It made him sad that these exciting days were not being shared with them and that they thought that December was nothing more than the beginning of Winter.

He started to feel guilty being happy when so many other people weren't. He would later learn that Christmas time makes a lot of people in the world feel this way.

His plan was working, his little talks with his friends about their past days was waking up their hope a little. Each time he saw them they opened up a little more. He was slowly working it out, this is what he did. Some people can just see the answer but they can't explain how they get there.

He spent a lot of time looking at the books and the tapes. He wished he could buy everyone a story book and a music tape, that would make them happy forever and after. There were so many films. Would they ever stop making them? So many ways to tell a story, poems, songs, books, films. The creative people keep so many stories inside their heads and they like to share them with the world.

Every time Carl heard about a new film, he thought surely that that must be the last one. That they couldn't possibly keep making more and then they did and they would probably do so for more than ten years.

Into the sweets aisle he went and then he stopped in his tracks. This was it. Something clicked and he knew he was staring at this year's magic of Christmas. This is what would light them up again and get them through the Winter! He almost jumped into the air with joy and he let out a little whistle. In his mind he saw this set up on Christmas morning and he knew how to do it all. He had worked it out and he knew what he would do.

The morning walk was a good one. There was no weather that Carl and his dad would not walk in. The day to a walk is every day that you go for a walk.

"It really smells like Christmas now everywhere we go" Carl said, "It feels cold enough to be Christmas."

It was a walk stopper. Carl now found that he too had a stare and that when he looked into it he could see things. He couldn't quite make out what he was seeing but he knew he had seen it.

"Yes, it does smell of Christmas," Dad said, "and it is cold enough for Christmas too. The seasons are changing and passing over the year. Do you want a small outdoor fire set up and have some baked potatoes and Chestnuts?"

Carl was instantly excited "Add a little hot chocolate and our Christmas tape and we have everything we need for the perfect memory."

Carl's Dad looked at him. He was so lucky to have a warm happy loving son. He was born to make life better. He was born to light up the darkness of Winter.

Carl stared into the fire. He was getting good at this staring magic now. He was smiling and shaking inside with his new plan. He liked it more knowing that his dad was not going to be in on it. It was such a great surprise that no one but himself could do it. He was in full control and he loved it. He felt that giving and making people happy was a part of Christmas that you had to make special yourself and enjoy.

Two wooden stools came outside and Carl's Dad read out a few wintery poems into the cold night. Samuel Taylor Coleridge was a favourite, Carl loved to read poetry but he liked to hear it even more. Especially when his dad would read it. Samuel Taylor Coleridge's poems sounded so magical when his dad read his words and thoughts. A Frost At Midnight had a nice opening line that Carl loved to hear every time.

"Poets know everything." said Carl.

Dad agreed "They know everything we need to know."

"I would like to grow up and find that I am a poet," said Carl.

"Maybe you are," Dad said. "You have all the makings of a great thinker. You are just at the early stages."

"I love being by the fire and hearing words that they wrote so long ago." Carl felt the warmth from the flames against his face

His Dad did too "The magic of a fire and the power of

great words and thoughts is with us from the early days to now. Gathering around a fire, telling stories if you can, and if you can't you have to listen to learn. You have to look after your family and friends around the fire."

Carl joined in "and if you can, you look after the whole village?"

"You do and if everyone does this, well, this is what we are here to do."

The days were all filled with the magic of Christmas. Although there was nothing more to be added to the plan Carl thought about it a lot. He never paused to think that something could go wrong. He was young enough to think more about what would go right. What needed done was being done and it was exciting to do.

He walked short walks along the stream and around the pond. He would let his dad go off ahead a little and he would add a little more magic into his bag but not say a word. Then he would take it into the old shed. There was nothing in there and no need to use it other than for secrets. The newer shed was bigger, better and used more by his dad.

And finally, it was here, the last paper round before Christmas, along with his papers the Christmas edition TV Guide was ready to deliver. Carl went through the village all smiles. He still had his secret to keep and had to say nothing to any of his friends about the surprise. He knew that no matter how hard they stared they could not see his secret.

He was going to wake them all up.

"Happy Christmas, Ted. I hope you have fun looking through the tv guide."

"I will, I will. Ted laughed and handed Carl a Christmas card.

"Oh, how kind of you. This is so nice. Can I take it home for my dad to see?"

"It is yours; you can do what you like."

"Happy Christmas, Tom."

"Here you go, two cakes for you and your dad."

"Oh, this is so kind."

"I have made it all Christmas in the cake box for you."

"Thank you, Thank you!"

Tom dropped the paper onto the kitchen table and made up a pot of tea. The TV Guide was a nice day in his life. By the morning fire with a pen he sat planning his tv week. James Bond was something Tom would only watch at Christmas and the search for the showing was on.

"Happy Christmas, Brian."

"Happy Christmas to you Carl. Do you think you will get any sleep?"

"I don't know. I have not needed any sleep for this month."

"Your whole life is a dream, Carl." Brian smiled at the happiest boy alive.

He later sat with his pipe and slowly opened the TV Guide. He flicked through, not wanting the pages to end. He stopped when he caught sight of the comedy duo, Cannon & Ball on Christmas Eve at 5.15pm

"Happy Christmas, Bill."

"Thank you, son." Bill knew now why he was a soldier for all of those years. It was for this boy. The life in Carl was the life in everyone. Every day seemed worth living that little bit more.

He poured a drink and took a seat at the table with his pen and he opened his TV Guide.

"Happy Christmas, Shane."

Carl laughed when he noticed the whole garden was dressed for Christmas, lights and tinsel covered his house and garden. It looked so magical.

"Do you like it?" Shane lifted his hands into the air. "I did it for you but once it was done, I loved it too!"

"Happy Christmas, Sue."

"And to you dear boy." She handed over a gift, it was covered and wrapped up for the big day but she knew that it was a painting of a loving man walking into the distance with his loving son. This walk would never end. A walk to nowhere and a walk with everything.

Sue poured a cup of tea by the fire and opened up her TV Guide. This day never failed to fill her with Christmas joy no matter how low she thought she was going to be. She smiled when she saw that The Snowman was going to be shown and she read the first page to see times and days to look forward to. A lot of magic comes from the screen and all the imaginations of the people making this all happen.

"Happy Christmas, Barnes!"

"It is indeed. You have a great day, Carl."

Barnes had covered his boats in Christmas lights. He looked on, happy and proud.

"This is brilliant. I love it! Christmas boats, what a great idea!" Carl loved the look on Barnes face

"Just added some lights to what already looked great to me." Barnes said bashfully.

"It's perfect,". Carl said, "Here you go." he handed over the paper and the TV Guide.

"I think you should check out the tv guide sitting in the main Christmas boat."

"You know." Barnes stopped to take this in. "I think I will."

"Happy Christmas, Ken."

"You too Carl. It has been a great end to the year. The village loves the new paperboy."

"I love the village! I have made so many nice new friends

and they have taught me a lot."

"No, it's you who has taught them a lot, you are a pocket full of magic Carl."

When Carl left the shop Ken smiled and carried on looking through the Christmas addition of the TV Guide. This would always be a part of so many peoples Christmas.

Carl parked up his bike and walked over to see Joan with her newspaper and tv guide. She looked like she had been crying.

"Happy Christmas, Joan. I have your paper."

"Thank you." she smiled a thin smile and held back more tears pushing her lips tightly together.

"I have your tv guide too. It is great to look through and circle the things that you like."

The smile broke and a little laugh escaped. "Yes. It is. Our lives are like tv guides in a way."

"We need more circles." Carl said

"We do." Joan let out a laugh at this incredibly happy boy. "We can circle wherever you are on any day at any time."

"That is nice. You are a circle to me too". Carl replied

Joan took a deep breath "I am not sure where you came from Carl but I am pleased that you arrived. You must hold onto the light that you are, the magic that you have and the hope that you give."

Carl shrugged. He had no idea how different he was and how only the good parts of life filled his heart. He knew no badness and sadness was not welcome in his life.

Joan cried when she turned into the house with her paper and tv guide. She was worried about Carl being in this world. They needed to protect him. He was worth fighting for.

Carl sat by the fire with his dad and they looked through their TV Guide together. A few circles were added already around Yogi's First Christmas, The Snowman, Christmas Racoons, Christmas Top of the Pops and Winnie the Pooh. Later a whole lot more would be added.

Carl and his dad finished reading A Christmas Carol. Ate some winter soup and played some Draughts and Ludo together. Keeping scores of all the games in a notebook.

Carl also noted down some of the stories his dad had told about life before Carl and life with Carl.

The logs burned away and more were added and the night lived on and on. The songs on the radio were of today and years gone by. Every one filled the room with happiness. Everything was feeling right and everything went to plan. The days were all repeated, filled with music, more decorations, baking, cooking, tv, reading. The kitchen was a place of magic but without Carl and his dad it was a kitchen in a cottage in a village in Northumberland.The morning of Christmas arrived once again and the people in the village woke with a smile, all with meaning but some more than others. They had made it to this day again and felt the happiness from Carl beaming through. He had opened them up once again and they were going to enjoy it. They would continue to do so for more years to come now that it was with them. What a wonderful start to their day knowing that Carl was happy in his magical world. The way that life should be, too many worries are brought into everyday life. Making people happy is the reason we are here. This is always something nice to learn.

Ted was up before the others. His life was always about early starts and later finishes. He slowed when he saw the card on the floor. He picked it up and left it on the table where he would have his giant Christmas day breakfast next to his TV Guide.

Tom looked down at the card and his smile was growing. It is always nice to receive a Christmas card knowing that someone has been thinking of you and taken the time to write it and get it to you on time. He picked up the card and dropped it on the chair where he would have a cup of tea and some toast and see what the morning TV had for him. He liked TV in December; it was good company and made him laugh and cry at all the right times

Brian picked up the card. He held it a while and realised he was not thinking, not asking questions, just standing holding a card, he was ready to start the day. He took the card to the kitchen and made up his breakfast.

At first Shane didn't see his card as he didn't pass the front door. But he would notice it when he took a look out into the garden to see what the morning of Christmas looked like this year.

Sue picked up the card and opened it straight away. She

did as the card told her and opened up the door and took in the morning freshness. It felt like she had been woken from a warm stuffy night and into a bright new cold but sunny morning. Once again, she stared but this time, she stared at something that was right there before her.

Elaine picked up the card and held it close to her and kept it there for a long time. She had a look of hope as she tried guessing who it would be from. She had met a lot of people in her life but not many of them sent cards, especially these days.

Barnes whistled a Christmas Carol as he walked down the stairs all set for another Christmas at home. He knew he wouldn't know the words even after all of these years but he did like to whistle, especially on Birthdays and Christmas Day. He stopped when he saw the card on the floor by the front door. "Oh, how nice."

Joan woke up and set the kettle to boil. Today would be toast and jam. If the day was dry and cold, she would drink the tea in the garden and like Carl said, look back on the nice days she had been a part of. This should be a nice day.

As she walked to the door, she saw the letter. She stared at the phone on the table by the door and waited for it to ring. It didn't. She did not want to spend another day hoping that someone would call her. It had never happened before so why would it today. Then she walked over and took the phone off the hook. Knowing that it wouldn't ring made her happy. "There, no one will call and I will spend the day looking back and forward and making plans." she liked this idea.

So, she picked up the letter, feeling funny, like everything was different.

"Happy Christmas my friend. I have left you a present outside at the door because I know that breaking in wouldn't be a good idea. I hope you like it. Love from Carl."

Joan opened the door. On the floor was a shoebox. She picked it up and took it through into the Kitchen.

She had to go slowly to let her tears clear. This was the most happiness she could remember in a long time. The others were all feeling this same way too. This was their Christmas in their own homes. Carl had done it, he had lit up the village, lit up their homes and lit up their lives.

Inside the box was some toffee with a hammer, bought from Woolworths. An orange, a small bag of nuts with a nutcracker, a bauble from the garden centre. A Gingerbread bell, a candy cane and notebook and a pen.

Then…. the best gift of all, a mixtape. Carl had made them all a Christmas mixtape.

Joan picked up the box like it was a baby, put in the music tape and danced around with the bundle of happiness, love and hope in her arms, in her life.

****

It had been 30 years since Carl woke the village up. He looked out of the old cottage window with his tape playing and the tv guide on the kitchen table. In his hand he held hot coffee knowing that later he would have his hot chocolate. This cottage was magic, he knew that it was himself and his father that had made it so magical. He had learned a lot of things in his life. He was a thinker and thinkers think. He was a lover and lovers love. He was a carer, he was a believer and what he knew was that we are here for each other. He was a poet and a poet knows everything worth knowing.

He remained a villager and lived in the house that Barnes had left behind for him. His work was to make sure people had food and shelter all year round. He never needed to be paid a penny as the whole village wanted to make sure that Carl never had to move away from his village and his life there. He was able to travel around setting up shelter for people without homes of their own. He had just been away for the last time before Christmas, he was a little later than usual but he was always on time.

He stared up at the field and smiled his everlasting smile. How many times had he walked these fields and stopped at the stream and the pond? The fire wasn't lit in the kitchen. Carl felt the cold but it didn't bother him. He loved every season. He belonged in them all.

He could see his dad walking through the field on this Christmas eve just like he had done through every year of Carl's life. The best walk of the year after the first walk of Autumn.

He ran out of the door and kept his eyes on him. Tears

welling. The hard mud frozen and crunching under his feet. He loved that sound.

There was never a feeling like this for Carl, many came close, but this stirred up Carl's first memories of life.

Life was supposed to be tough but they had made it work. Teamwork had done it. If you play for the team, you can win. Should one of you fall then there will be enough help around you to get you back up.

Nicholas turned his head, his white hair and beard blowing in the wind. He caught sight of his son running towards him, just as he had done his whole life. He loved to see his smile and hear the joy as Carl arrived by his side. He had with him boxes ready to fill with Christmas for the rest of the village. No one wakes up to nothing because they all believe in something.

Carl had filled him with everlasting happiness and hope in a time when nothing made sense. There was no fear or sadness allowed in this heart, in this village.

THE END

Three Winter Tales

.

Three Winter Tales

ONION SOUP

Today was the most perfect and wonderful day in the world for Marvin. The sun was up in the sky where it belonged and the frost was on the ground where the morning dew had surrendered to the cold and turned to crystals. It could not have looked or felt more magical. It was perfect.

He stood at the door and took it all in. The world looked like it should and all was calm.

His mother dropped the onions into the large brown sack whilst his Father added his daily dance to the day. He was as happy and proud of the onions that he had grown as he was with his son's task of the day.

"Now you be careful on the way," his mother said, "no falling down and rolling into rivers" she handed him a bottle of water and two apples for the journey. One for Marvin and one for his friend, Max.

Max would be waiting on the wooden seat in the warmth of the sun and the cold of the Winter. Marvin loved these happy days. Even though he was still young they reminded him of his earlier years in his life. He knew that he would always remember these days. He had listened to the stories of his father and his father's father and his father too. The stories all had the same theme, every one filled with happiness and smiles.

His mother fussed about him some more, "You know the way by now, we will be there to join you all later tonight."

They would all be there for the big catch up with food and more stories.

"I will be careful, I promise, I'll follow our tradition and make it on time. I'll be nice and early too, so that nobody at the other end worries about it all being late. Being late is not in our plans, is it Dad?" said Marvin, quoting one of his father's favorite phrases.

"Better to be a warrior than a worrier." his dad spoke softly through a smile.

"I'm a warrior just like you"

"Only much better!" Dad threw one more onion to Marvin and he caught it. He could feel the energy from the moment.

Marvin did this walk last year with his father. This year he was allowed to walk alone or with a friend, sharing good things with friends was his favorite thing to do, so of course he asked Max.

Marvin and Max were born on the same day, their parents had been great friends before but they were even greater friends now. The Fathers worked together as the village gardeners and were always "full of busy". They loved looking after everyone and making sure they kept the village tidy. Keeping people happy made them feel happy too. Marvin and Max helped them out most weeks but they also got a lot of free time, time to grow up. Walking, exploring and fishing were high on their favorite things to do list.They lived every day like a great adventure because for them it was.

The morning had not been here long. It was the very start of the day and to Marvin this was always exciting. He didn't want to miss a minute of light. The night had ended less than an hour ago.

It was very bright but with his glasses tinted to help from the glare and his giant straw hat he was able to enjoy the sunny days. There was always so much to see, to hear, to smell, taste and touch.

Max was dressed in the same way as Marvin, he always was. He was so interested in everything around him that he was usually late to wherever he was supposed to be.

"Good morning." said Max, waving with both hands excitedly.

"And a good morning to you and to us and to all who are awake right now. It is hard to believe that these mornings can be missed. They are so special."

"Do you think those that don't see the morning are sad to have missed it?"

"They don't know what they are missing or maybe they have seen a morning and thought that it was'.... boring." They both laughed.

Max ran and slid over an iced over puddle. "Boring? I don't see what is ever boring about a morning or any time of the day."
"We are all here for different things I suppose." Marvin nodded slowly. He was a big reader and always thinking. He sometimes said things that were so great he would be in disbelief at what he had just come out of his mouth. If you can impress yourself then you can impress anyone.

Max picked up a stick, broke it in two and played a beat on the fence like a rock and roll drummer. He was in the zone, enjoying the sounds he was adding to what would have just been silence. His head nodded and his eyes were closed.

"How are the lessons going?" asked Marvin.

"I am a natural. Better than anyone before me probably. Who knows?"

"It's so good to know that my best friend could travel around playing the drums with all of the best bands in the world."

"I could just do it on my own if I wanted," Max replied, shrugging. "I'm good enough!"

"Oh"Marvin asked," Wouldn't you prefer to be in a band?"

"I don't know. I don't want anyone holding me back, you know." He already had the confidence of a rock star.

Marvin's father stood at the doorway. "That is a fine beat you have going there."

"Yes, it is." replied Max.

Marvin's mother came out to listen. Hand in hand his parents started to dance around on the frosty ground beneath them. Marvin clapped and nodded too. Laughter filled the morning air. Every second looked like a Christmas card.

Once the dance was done Marvin's father took a wooden barrow from the shed and pushed it onto the dirt track "Are you ok with the barrow?"

Marvin replied, "Yes, it is slower but it's easier to manage, we are early and there is no great hurry."

"You are right, son, it is always nice to be able to take your time. Take in as much of each day as you can for as many days as possible throughout your wonderful happy life."

Max tested the barrow. "I can help, this is not heavy at all, even with two sacks of onions."

Side by side they waved and set off all full of life. They had the same overwhelming feeling as waking up and realizing it's Christmas day.

Kevin ran through trees, a long red-haired blur. He was always very quiet for one moving so fast. He grinned as he ran down onto the path with his red sack and dropped it on the ground.

"I am so excited. Are you two going to hurry up?"

Marvin and Max beamed, for them, Kevin's entrance was like hearing the opening chord of a band at a long-awaited festival, a rush of excitement waved over them both.

Max replied, "We are taking our time, Kevin. This is a day to remember for everyone and we have the onion duty so we are very important. We want to fill the day with memories along the way as well as later on when we are all together.".

"I am happy that you get to enjoy the walk with a friend. I prefer to be on my own. I don't like being slowed down." Even Kevins words came out fast,

"You go ahead then and we will meet you at the fire." added Marvin.

"Yes, yes. You are right, I can't wait around. I'll run ahead and meet you there."

Within seconds he was away through the trees where he could no longer be seen or heard.

"It is sad that Kevin is always on his own." Max picked up a pine cone and threw it up into the air and caught it one handed. He looked over to Marvin to see if he was as impressed as he was.

"He likes to be on his own, making camps and hiding in the woods is how he likes to be. If he didn't like being alone, he wouldn't be alone. "

"As long as he is happy then he can do whatever he likes. I must say I do prefer to have a friend to be with in my life."

"We are lucky that we like being friends," said Marvin with a big smile. "I like to be happy"

"Can I always be happy with you?" Max tilted his straw hat as he waited for his reply.

"You can always be happy with me. It is what friends are here for, for each other. Everyone on this earth has the job to make friends. There is always someone waiting and needing to be a friend. It never ends." Marvin picked up a pine cone and flipped it to Max, he caught it.

William walked down onto the path with a bundle of sticks wrapped in string. He always wore his tweed cap and magic waistcoat and always big boots. Even though he was always happy he rarely looked like it until he spoke.

"Good morning, Bill," said Marvin.

"Good morning! This is a very special one. I am so proud to be a part of it, so nice to be invited."

"That is a lot of sticks. Have you been picking them all morning?" said Max.

"I collect them when I'm walking through the Autumn months. Sticks and berries too. I do love walking through the seasons. Watching and tasting them as they change."

"Oh, I love berry jam." said Max excitedly picking up another pine cone and placing it onto the wooden cart.

"There will be plenty of jam tonight! There will be plenty of everything." William stopped to look over the water between the river banks. "The look of a river is my favorite sight. The sound of a stream is my favorite sound. Feeling like this is my favorite feeling."

Marvin and Max walked over and stood by William and took in the wise river. The frost and the red berries are the look of Winter for so many. The broken branches did not look out of place in this scene.

"The stream must turn into a river before it reaches the sea and is lost in the big water. What a journey." William closed his eyes and remembered the times that he had stood by the river to feel its silent power as it moved towards the sea.

The Robin flew in close, just out of reach but in sight as usual and for not too long, after a quick look, it was off again. This whole scene lasted a few seconds and could have been missed in a blink.

William saw what looked to be a wizard. He smiled and walked on a few steps. "Look, there is the Wizard standing still in the distance. He rarely speaks and is always alone. He knows everything." He looked a while longer, waiting for nothing to happen but to feel some kind of magic from the wizard.

Max and Marvin watched the Wizard too. He was very still and demanded silence without saying a word. There was something magical about the moment and no one wanted to break the spell or the silence. He tried hard to stay quiet but eventually Max interrupted. "How do we know that the wizard knows everything if he has no friends and never speaks?"

"He keeps all the knowledge to himself; he needs no information from others. He knows everything he needs to know and that is all that we need to know." replied William.

Marvin had pulled down his straw hat a little at the sides to protect himself from the shouting that never arrived.

"He knows the answer to everything." William said knowingly." He has memories from the past stored away for the future. Wizards like to be left alone unless it is about something important. I talked to the Wizard a long time ago, you only ever need to talk to a wizard once"

"Fishing is my important thing?" said Max in a low whisper.

"That is a good thing" said William "I'm sure the wizard knows all about fishing. Whenever I think about fishing it immediately creates a happy scene in my head."

"Mine too." smiled Max.

William appeared to snap back to the moment "Ok, I think it is time for you two to move on. Stick to the path and get to where you are going. Not too quick but not too slow."

They carried on a little further and only stopped when they reached a large green sack of carrots. They took a look around until Colin and Lucy appeared from the woods with a second large sack.

"Hello you two, how nice to meet up on our little adventure." Lucy said, moving in close to Max and Marvin. "How has it been for you so far?" She had a smile for everyone, one that the whole world could see if they were looking.

"We are so excited, it's nice to see all of the carrots. They look so big and so many." Marvin replied.

"We have a lot more back home." said Colin, nodding, "Back through the trees and up the hill, you can never have too many carrots! They should be a part of everyone's day and night, not just ours."

Marvin picked up the sack to feel just how heavy it was. "Oh my, this is so heavy."

"It makes it all more worth doing if there is a struggle on the way." Colin said as he swung the sack onto his back and added a leaping side kick to the moment. "Meet you at the end." he added and off he went. Lucy jumped with joy and also added a side kick before letting out a little noise of excitement, she caught up with Colin in seconds.

The pathway looked magical. The trees on the left side, the river on the right and the shady parts all frosted, sparkly and inviting. Colin and Lucy were not left in sight for long. They didn't like to be seen very often but, on this day, like everyone, they enjoyed the company of the ones they rarely saw or heard for the rest of the year.

"This time of the year comes around so fast" Marvin said to his friend" I am pleased we are still new to this life!"

"Time is for everyone and time is for no-one. You have to make the most of time and make it your own. Oh, I could go on but I get bored of myself when I get like this." Simon laughed a gentle laugh.

Max and Marvin stopped and looked around. They recognised the voice which was owned by a face so few ever saw. Simon stepped out from behind the trees. Thin, tall and looked like an athlete, indeed he once was an athlete but that was some summers ago now. At his side was his yellow sack, tied with a red ribbon.

"Have you had a nice year?" Marvin asked him politely.

"Most of it was good and some of it was even better. I do like to fill my year with things that make me happy. There is so much happy to find, be sure you get it found."

"Surely everyone already does this." added Max.

"Well, you would think so but so few do. There is always more good to find in life so I like to keep on looking for it. The search keeps me busy and being busy keeps me searching."

"You are always happy," said a grinning Marvin.

"I am always searching." Simon picked up a stick and in the frosted mud he drew a snowman.

"That's great." said Marvin as he stared without blinking until it was finished.

"A snowman," said Simon looking up, all proud. "In the mud, a Snowman."

"I think you made a Mudman?" laughed Max.

"Yes, mud is always mud be it wet, dry or frosted." Simon picked up his sack. "See you at the end and have a nice walk but remember, we will all be waiting so don't be late." and before they knew it he was off up the track and out of sight leaving Max and Marvin smiling, admiring the snowman and waiting for it to move. It didn't but something else did.

Ben walked up behind them dragging a cart of sticks and

logs. He had made the cart himself. Ben made everything himself. This is how it had always been in his family, if you want something then you make something.

Ben's voice was calm, he was too, he was also very tall. "Good morning Max, good morning Marvin, a very good morning it is too. The world is dry and it's cold enough to be warmed once I get the fire going." Ben loved making a fire, the sticks, the branches, the logs.

"Oh Ben" Marvin exclaimed, "we are so looking forward to all being together and hearing the stories, listening to poems and eating food until there is nothing left. You add so much to the night, everyone always tells me this."

"Nice to know. I see you have the onions, there is no soup without onions and there is no feast without soup."

"Does it take long to get the fire going?" asked Marvin.

"No, the fire never takes long, as long as the wood is dry. I keep the wood I gather in a shed so that it can be dry enough." Simon handed them both a chunk of peppermint that he had wrapped in a small paper bag.

"Oh, thank you, Ben." Max took his chunk and looked over at the wide-eyed Marvin. "Winter is such a special time for sharing and keeping each other warm." his mouth watering as he brought his chunk up to his mouth for his first bite.

"Pick up a few of the pinecones. They are good for the fire." Ben suggested.

"Yes, we will add a few into our sack." Max pushed the

rest of the peppermint into his mouth and set about picking up a few of the surrounding pinecones. He looked out into the silent running water. His eyes closed as he was overwhelmed with his warm surroundings on such a cold day.

"I will meet you at the end." Ben shouted" It is nice to see you both so happy and well. Remember this day, you can use it any time." he moved on ahead dragging the sticks and logs on his cart behind him.

Mr and Mrs Chance were returning to the fire. It was not yet lit but the wood that had been brought was stacked in separate piles of sticks, branches and logs. There was enough to have a fire for a long time.

The sticks and branches were tied in bundles with string. The couple were as busy as ever and as usual they were so busy that they didn't have much to say.

"Good morning, so nice to see you both with so many fine onions. Marvin, I will tell your father that he has done very well growing them once again. It's time now to add all of the tasty vegetables to the pans. Hand them over boys and we will get to it." Mr Chance did not want a reply. He had said what he wanted to say and was so busy in the moment that he could think of nothing else. He caught up with his wife who was rushing about too. Their large brown matching coats made you feel warm from simply looking at them.

"See you later boys. "Mr Chance called over his shoulder.

"I always thought it was just onions in the soup," said

Max.

"No," Marvin said," that is what we personally add to the soup. I believe that a lot of others think this way too. That whatever they add to the soup is all it needs to make it great, but it isn't true. We all add something different, all of our own skills, experiences and tastes."

"Onion Soup with vegetables," said Max with a smile. They stopped to fist pump. Max threw a stone into the river and he stared at the water lost in thought.

"Do you know where this river leads, Max?"

"The sea?" he replied, holding a thought stance.

"Eventually but before you get there."

Max shook his head."Some say that it is where a great badger, a rat, a toad and a very nice mole still live."

Ben walked over at just this moment and paused as he reached their sides. "And some of us just know it is," he added. "They are always here somewhere." Ben smiled as he joined them to walk over the little wooden bridge to cross the river. He waved over to the wizard. Even though the wizard stayed very still, Ben knew he was not being ignored because that is what Herons do.

****

"Look! I see them!" cried a boy as he ran to his father and he dragged him a little closer by the hand. Just as his dad expected, there were two moles wearing matching straw hats walking along with a sack on a wagon.

"I told you it was true," the father beamed. "If you never tell anyone then you can come here every year on this day just as I have."

The boy just about burst with the magic of nature. His eyes lit up and he punched the air with two clenched fists. The moles were catching up to two beavers that were carrying bundles of sticks. Up near the top of the hill there was a small fire and a large cooking pot. Two rabbits were unpacking carrots from a green sack as a robin watched over them. A squirrel jumped from a nearby tree with a red sack over its shoulder. The hare stood over a yellow sack, tall and proud.

****

That was the first time I saw the animals at their annual gathering. I have never missed one since.

This is the magic I take through each year, like my father and his father and it never ends. No matter where I am in my life, I am one dream away from waking up. Beside the river with all of the happiness, hope and magic that one child needs to get through life. We are never alone as long as we know that we are never alone.

I was told never to speak a word of this to anyone and I have not. Just you.

THE END

Three Winter Tales

Three Winter Tales

DEAR SANTA

Laura was tired, but not for very long. She was always tired around the busy season. It was the dark cold night outside and the warm house heated by the log fire that made her feel tired or like most people in the winter call it, cozy.

Today was a special day in the most special season. A time when many people are "cozy" and busy.

In the mirror she brushed through her golden hair and blinked her sparkling blue eyes just before showing her teeth with a very happy smile. This smile was made by her very happy life. A smile can forever change the mood of the person you are showing it to, even if it is just your own self. I suggest to you all to smile more.

Christmas Eve was not just a busy time for Laura but for Mam, Dad, Granny and Grandad and probably. A day for a lot of other people to make happy memories and make each other happy, not only for Winter but for ever and ever.

At 9 years old Laura was making the most of single figured life by being around the people that she loved the most. She didn't know how lucky she was to be here right now with all of these wonderful magical people and although she knew that she meant a lot to them she didn't realise quite how much.

School was over for the holidays; her friends would be there waiting for her when she returned but for now it was family time. For now, it was Christmas.

She wore her Christmas red dress. It was tradition for her to wear a new one every year. This year it was patterned with tiny Christmas trees, last year had been patterned with bells, the year before candy canes. Granny made a new dress every year which made it even more special.

Today her shoes and her wellies would take turns protecting her feet and adding a little extra height to her day, which every growing child likes. Finding out you have grown a little taller means a lot, especially on a birthday, we all grow a little more on our birthdays, right?

The Christmas songs were playing on the radio as they had been for the whole of December. Each one adding uncontrollable smiles to the listeners.

Laura walked in just as Grandpa was adding wood to the fire, his smile was just as warm as the room and could easily last until Springtime, maybe longer? a whole lifetime!

"Good morning." she cried out almost in song.

"It is. Are you ready for your day? You look as beautiful and as happy as ever."

"Thank you, Grandpa. You look as handsome and as happy as ever."

Grandma walked in from the kitchen. "I am ready when you are." she said.

Laura walked into the kitchen and washed her hands. Everything was ready for baking. On the table there were different shaped cutters and glass bowls with the already measured out ingredients. Plain flour, ground ginger, butter, syrup, muscovado sugar, bicarb of soda and eggs. They mixed and cut out shapes ready to go in the oven. As they stirred the different coloured icing, the smells of Christmas mingled with their excited chatter. Only the loud "ping" of the oven would interrupt them when the gingerbread was baked.

Grandpa came in just as Laura finished adding the smiling faces and raisin buttons to the characters and Grandma had tidied the dishes away. He got to work on making breakfast for everyone.

Grandma and Grandpa lived next door but they shared both houses. They shared everything in life so Christmas was always going to be a close, shared magical time.

After breakfast a walk was walked with Laura, Grandpa and her father. They took shovels to clear away snow from other driveways in the street. They were not the only ones with this idea, many people in the street cleared their own and the houses around them too. They were all in it together. A kindness like this adds a little fun and a little Christmas Eve cheer too.

If we all did a little more than just our own drive, life could be better for everyone.

Some people had left out Christmas cake, cookies and gingerbread. The smell of Christmas and the look of love was all around. Drinks were poured to anyone wanting one. Hot and cold. Music played as Elton John was asking everyone to step into Christmas.

This is how Laura's family lived, they cared about each other, this is all they knew and nothing would change. Laura's future and traditions were being paved by her past just as it had been for all of her family.

There was no snow on the beach and Laura ran over the sand, she stopped from time to time to pick a few shells to take home for the memories. Shiny stones were dropped into her pockets too. The sea looked so innocent dancing to a song she knew but nobody could hear.

You should never have to be brave when you are a child. Dance and sing forever, someone will always join in.

All year round the family walked the sands collecting driftwood so that Mother could make the most wonderful crafts, framed fish and short driftwood Christmas Trees.

This is the place where poems are found. The poets always know where to find poetry, we should always listen to them, they know things that cannot always be taught. Wherever the wind blows is a magical place for thought catching.

In the sand Laura used a stick to draw a Christmas tree and to write Merry Christmas.

Hand in hand with her Grandad Laura walked up the wooden steps onto the track back to their home not a two-minute walk from the village. They all had tears in their eyes from the wind.

"This will help you to sleep tonight my little Laura." Grandad always talked slowly, this was because he knew everything and he meant every word.

He always looked happy and calm. He lived the life he wanted to live from the age of understanding and he looked like a rock star from the 1960s. His Long grey hair was tight in a ponytail. He had a face that told everyone that he knew the way, they knew to either stay out of his way or follow him. They also knew never to ask questions that do not need answering. (These rules did not apply to Laura).

Her Father looked like a 90s rock star and played guitar. Laura was lucky to live the life she lived surrounded by people who understood happiness.

Up onto her father's shoulders she felt the cold on her face. He moved fast passing the small pond, it looked asleep and would be until Spring. Not many weeks went by without a visit to the pond.

He followed the stream to the bottom of their garden where they were all welcomed back into the house and into the log burning kitchen.

The Christmas songs played on but the radio was louder than it was earlier. The extra Crepe paper decorations were only crafted and added on the 24th but the houses in the village had all been dressed up since the end of Autumn.

Laura sat at the kitchen table and coloured in pictures with her grandmother as her mother continued folding colourful paper. This was magic memory time and they all knew it.

Wizzard sang out "I Wish It Could Be Christmas Every Day" and everyone joined in with the chorus, even though Laura and her grandma laughed that every day would be a little too much.

The candles were ready for later when the sun went down to wherever it goes before waking everyone on Christmas day.

Laura went out with her mother and her grandmother with the pictures she had coloured in throughout the year. 47 Christmas pictures for the people of the village. It made them all smile; she understood what it meant more each year. Adding a little something to the lives of others and in turn adding some extra "happy" to her own life.

The cards had all been written and delivered on the 1st of December. Today was the final hello and goodbye before Christmas day.

Laura loved to see the decorations and taste some of the food left out for everyone. The village looked like Christmas. A sight worth waiting for all year.

Every door had a handmade wreath decorated with winter care and magic. Every garden had Christmas ornaments. Reindeer, Snowmen, Santa, Elves, Candy Canes. (I know, you get it). The magic of people in Winter makes for a happier, warmer place, wherever you are.

Every house was lit up. The feeling was warm as you walked the village.

Once Laura had delivered 46 of the pictures her father turned up pulling a sledge, more just for fun this year. Laura would be pulled up the hill to Mrs Miller's house near the top. It was a mighty big hill for a mighty small child.

Mrs Miller was a friendly lady and well worth all of the effort, like most people here she grew up in the village. Her husband was a toy maker when he was around, he had made so many toys all out of wood, enough for decades of children to have a toy on Christmas Eve. Every day had been toy making day.

"Merry Christmas, little Laura. She said pleasantly from her lit up doorway. The smell of food carried in the wind from her warm cosy house. The heat and the smells were enough to send you to a dreamy sleep on your feet.

"Happy Christmas to you." Laura ran up to the door with the picture. Mrs Miller held up the picture and smiled. "Thank you, you get better every year my dear young thing."

Laura beamed "I love colouring in my pictures for you all."

"It shows! A lot of care has gone into this colouring." Mrs Miller handed over a wooden toy to Laura. "Someone made this for you, he also liked to take care and add his love to everything that he made." She smiled and a tear arrived with joy. As she watched she saw the little girl light up with the happiness and love that was put into the toy by her late husband. He would always be here on earth because he had left a part of himself in these toys.

Laura stood by her Father's side looking up at the grown-ups' eyes as they talked about times gone by, when he was a boy living in the village and even earlier when she was a little girl. It is important that you make as many wonderful memories as you can and then there is more to look back on. If you are lucky enough to share them with someone then it is even better.

They accepted some cherry cake and ate it as they talked. The visit to see Mrs Miller was nice and it was always worth staying a little longer. She was good company and it was nice to be company for her. Her cherry cake was the finest around, coupled with hot chocolate it was perfect. Especially as the milk was heated over a flame and served in a Christmas beaker that Mrs Miller said Laura could keep.

Laura was on the sledge being pulled home to be with the family once again to slowly end the night. She closed her eyes as she glided across Winter's blanket. There would never be another feeling to compare this to in her life.

Once home Laura sat by the fire with her wooden toy dog. The heat from the flames connected her to our ancestors, not only feeling warm but safe too.

She put on some Christmas cartoons and let the grown-ups do what they had to do before they all settled down for a Christmas movie.

She watched "Chip and Dale", "Donald Ducks Winter Storage", "Pluto's Christmas tree" and laughed as Micky taught Minnie his ice-skating skills. Laura loved all cartoons but the ones that had meaning to her family meant more to her too. They shared the hours by the fire watching tv. She enjoyed seeing them smile at the past as the cartoons made them remember their own childhoods.

The light of the day was over now, only man-made light lit up the village. The logs were still burning on the fire and Grandma waited until the cartoons and movie were over, signaling that the big day had ended by taking out her favourite book, "A Christmas Carol".

Laura loved anyone reading a story to her, each different person made it their own.

Laura's Mother sat down and cuddled close so she could listen to her own Mother reading just as she had done her whole life.

The smells in the house were a mixture of all of the smells of Christmas, the food, the tree and the candles.

There were so many lights and decorations collected over the decades that many memories surrounded them. The house was filled with love and the magic of Winter. Tomorrow was the big day, the weeks leading up to the big day had all been special, the more effort they put into Christmas, the greater it became.

Time moved on, the seconds taking the minutes by the hand just as Grandma took Lauras. It was time to leave the day, tomorrow was waiting and they were all as ready as they could be. She turned off their background music and led Laura to the window to see the magic of Christmas as the snow fell onto the snow. The silence lasted a lifetime. They both turned at the same time and smiled.

"Shall we get a hot chocolate and sit in the garden?"

This idea was the best because it was new and made on the spot. Some moments need planning but not this one, it was right here and now and would be remembered. "Yes please." replied Laura. They heated milk and waited until it was ready. Wrapped up warm they walked out into the cold and the warmth of Winter.

The hot chocolate would not stay hot for long but it would keep its name. They sipped at the drink from the moment they walked outside. The taste of food and drink is always different when outside. It is almost like eating and drinking with our distant relatives from past days when family and food were the whole meaning of life.

The falling flakes took their time enjoying the soft fall before joining the others on the ground.

Grandma and Laura took a seat in the wooden shelter. Dad and Grandad made a lot of things together and this was one of their best ideas and works.

"I have so many wonderful Christmas Eves to look back on. I have written them down so I can remind myself of the past and maybe one day you can look at my past in your future."

"Oh, I would love to read your memories, Grandma. How very exciting."

"Then you will." she smiled. "I was your age when I started to write them."
And you still have all of this written down?"

"I do...once I even wrote a letter to Santa and asked if I could spend Christmas Eve with him to introduce him to my family and let him enjoy the Eve of the big day before whizzing off around the world."

Laura thought for a moment "He would be too busy."

"Well my dear, my thinking was that the elves play their part and on the 24th Santa rests whilst they get everything ready."

"I feel dizzy just thinking about it." Laura took another sip from the mug.

Her grandma told her "I titled the letter Christmas Wish, it was a wish for him, so that he could enjoy the day. It was never really for me, although I would have loved to spend the day with Santa even if it had to remain a secret forever and longer." She smiled; eyes closed as she looked back on this time from the past.

"Did you get a reply?"

Gran nodded. "I did, a beautiful letter came for me tied in ribbon, it said 'Sorry but as generous and wonderful as this sounds there is simply no time for this.'

Laura looked sad. "Oh, that must have been sad news."

Gran shook her head "No, the reply was enough. This Magic helped me to realise that we all have to make our homes ready for him coming down the chimney every year, If he puts in so much effort so should we. It gave me the magic I needed to carry me through every day of every year and every Winter to come. ."

"Who wrote the reply?" Laura said in a shocked voice.

"Mrs Clause."

Laura almost fell off the wooden stool. "You got a reply from Mrs Clause?"

"I did. "Grandma laughed with joy. "I did, my dear."

"Does everyone here know?" Laura whispered.

"They do. They all know the story."

Laura made up a snow ball and threw it into the air to catch it, she caught it and threw it back up into the air. "This is my favourite story. I am so happy that you shared it with me."

Grandma laughed gently "There are plenty more"

Laura looked at her ever happy Grandma who was still and looking down at the snow remembering the Christmas Eve stories that she had stored in her mind. Occasionally she smiled. She was floating in a magical stare.

Laura left her like this for a while before asking "Should we go in now and hear a song by Dad and Grandad?" Grandma nodded in agreement and they walked into the house, Dad was ready and strummed a chord on his acoustic guitar to check that it was in tune before they all sang together "Oh Christmas Tree".

The day had to end; it had been a tiring one. Usually when you are tired and happy tomorrow is never far away and the night can be over in a blink.

Laura didn't want to go to sleep and put an end to this day and all of its loving magic but she knew that when she next woke it would be Christmas day. So off she went for a cuddle and a kiss from her family. She brushed her teeth and one by one everyone took turns standing in the doorway to wish her a "Happy Christmas and good night". All but Grandma.

Laura couldn't sleep. She was remembering her grandma's face, hoping that it wasn't a glimmer of sadness that she had been showing. It did not suit her; it did not belong there.

Outside the snow still fell and she tried counting snowflakes until she went to sleep. It wasn't for long though as she kept waking up. This was new to Laura, usually, once asleep this is what she did until she woke up. A good night's sleep was every night for her. This broken sleep was new, again she drifted off but this time when she woke the cold took her breath away. She did not hear a sound but she felt a presence like someone else was awake in the house other than herself. She felt afraid.

The thought of Grandma being sad with a mug of hot chocolate came at her and pushed her bravely out of bed. Maybe Grandma was out of bed because she could not sleep either.

Laura took her dressing gown from the hanger on the door and walked down stairs. She did not try to sneak down, but she was still very quiet.

As she moved through the house she heard a sound from her living room, it was one she had never heard before, a sound that could only be described as magical. A feeling radiated from the open gap in the living room door, it felt clear and right, like all the good in the world was in here right now.

She pushed it open and looked towards the fireplace, the fire was no longer burning but set to be lit in the morning. It all happened so fast but there was a flurry and a blur as the calm happy magical feeling left in a magical breeze up the chimney.

That's when Laura noticed the tree surrounded by all of the gifts. She felt excited and worried, like she had broken the rules. She was now becoming aware of what she had done.

She had only come down to see Grandma, not seeing her was shocking enough but this!

"Oh no." she whispered. "What have I done? Have I broken a spell?"

She turned to see if there was anyone around, anyone coming down. Did anyone else hear the sound of magic, the sound of Christmas?

She closed her eyes, hoping to open them and be back safe in her own bed. She paused a while but the second she opened up her eyes she saw it. Quickly walking over, she picked it up. It was the biggest boot she had ever seen in her life, even in a book or in a film. This, she knew, was the boot of Santa and ducked inside it was a little character.

Laura gasped and threw the boot and its contents onto the floor "OK, OK, the little character said, " I'm Winston, please don't be scared or I will be forced to freeze you. It won't hurt but really you don't want to be frozen, It's so boring."

82

Laura nodded to show that she understood, but still took a few steps backwards, Winston explained that he was an elf, he spoke in a low but sharp voice. He looked like most elves do in the books, on tv and in the films, all dressed in green from hat to boots. In his hand he held a feather pen and he carried a clipboard. His face changed from very happy to very serious and he never seemed to hold the same expression for more than a few seconds.

Laura stood wide eyed, and felt the excitement from her toes explode as she jumped up into the air.

With his hand raised. "Please, Laura, stay calm. This is a busy night and I have to catch back up with Santa." He floated Laura back down to the ground using his magic.

"You know Santa?" she whispered.

Winston looked shocked, then shrugged. "Every elf knows Santa. Don't you ever read?" He rolled his eyes and started to pace the room.

"Sorry, I just don't know what to say."

"Then say nothing, that is what people do when they do not know what to say or at least they used to.

Now, pick the boot back up and hold your hand over it, I will write you your wish."

Laura did as he asked and picked up the giant boot. It was so shiny she felt it fill her with energy. She was sure that holding the boot of Santa was not something many, if any people got to experience. "What is my wish?" she asked.

"I don't know, do I! It is you who needs to know this! How am I supposed to know what you want to wish for! So come one, make a wish and make it now…. Come on…. wish. One wish now, make it!!!" Winston tapped his foot impatiently on the floor, tightened his lips and looked up at the top of the tree. "Come on!!"

"This is such a surprise; I think I need help to decide?"

"Well, what would you like? A bike, a book, a lifetime of nice dreams? I can do anything?"

Laura dropped back into the moment. "I have it."

"Tell, tell, tell." Winston sat on the floor by the tree ready to write out the wish.

"My Grandmother wrote a letter to Santa way before she was a grandmother."

"Yes, I know this, before she was even a mother. A little girl she was back then. He smiled and nodded slowly as he looked back on the moments in years gone by."

"Oh, do you remember?"

"Not exactly, it's a kind of magic, I just know things that I need to know."

"Can that be my wish? To let my Grandma, spend the day with Santa and let him see what our family life is like."

"If you want Grandma to spend the day with Santa then this is the wish that will come true."

"Just like that?"

"Yes. He has made a mistake tonight by leaving a boot on the scene to be seen. He was actually taking off his boots for a little rest and you disturbed him. He whizzed away and left it. You found it, anyone who sees Santa gets a wish or indeed anyone who finds his boot, which has never happened before. You have proof of Santa you see.

You can never tell anyone as no one will believe you so instead you get a wish as an apology from the man himself."

"Oh, my goodness, this is the greatest night of my whole life, Winston."

"You are just like her, you know. You are here for everyone. A child like you is very rare these days, or any day, a child like Penny, your grandma, was rare then. Do you know Penny raises money for people all year to make sure they are fed over Winter and kept warm. She sees to it all, just like Santa. She never wants anything in return, she just does what her heart asks of her and what so many people need."

Laura was surprised. "Oh, this is so nice to hear."

Winston handed her the wish written on a piece of paper. "You need to keep this to yourself. Your wish is written. Take it and hide it away for a whole year. No one can know or the wish will be broken. You have to let this whole night become your very own memory. Sadly, this is the way."

"I won't break the promise and I will make sure my grandma will get her wish."

"Ok, time to get to sleep so you can wake up to the magic and love of Christmas."

Winston smiled. "I have enjoyed meeting you, Granddaughter of Penny."

"I have loved meeting you too, Winston."

"Off you go. Have a nice sleep and then have a nice day tomorrow. Remember to make every day magical for all around you. Never let it stop and surround yourself with nice people. You will all look after each other and you will all be surrounded by happiness and hope. I know you know this now but it will get harder the more people you meet. Not all are as kind as you and your family."

"Can I hug you?" Laura asked.

Winston looked up to the skies and lifted his arms. "If you like."

They closed their eyes and took in the warmth of another life.

Laura climbed the stairs and jumped into bed. Winston dropped a handful of magic in the room to send her to sleep. The wish held tight in her hand was gone when she woke and the dream was over.

Christmas was everything they made of it. A wonderful day full of happiness and love. They took many photos with their minds and with all the cameras.

Taking it all in so that they could remember it forever.

Laura paused from time to time to remember her dream and looked at her grandma with fresh eyes. Her beautiful friend, Grandma Penny. Where had she been, what has she seen, what has she done?

All you need to know is that you are with each other now to enjoy your time together.

Laura kept an eye on her. She always looked happy but she also looked tired from time to time. So, Laura stayed close to let her know that she was not alone in anything and that she was loved and always needed and appreciated.

The day ended in the garden with hot chocolate again and everyone talked about the highlights of this year and previous Christmas times. Music played in the background but the volume got lower as the hours passed by.

Grandma tucked Laura in to end the day. Sleep was not far away. Nothing ever is.

The seasons came and went. The wind blew them in and the wind blew them away until once more the Autumn was coming to an end. December was back with everyone, for all of the people wanting to light up the Winter and give happiness and hope to family, friends and a few strangers. Light up the night, light up the Winter.

Laura was running home from a day of gathering pine cones. Later she would paint a few and put them at the entrance of the door. Once the tree had been put up in the living room the first of the Christmas songs played. David Essex sang how it was only a Winter's Tale, just another Winter's Tale.

It had been a great year, 11 busy and happy months and this was once again the "Thank You to Everyone" month. The end of a year, a time to look back before once again looking forward and doing it all again.

Laura never mentioned last Christmas Eve. It was no longer a secret, just a distant memory. A year is a very long time when you are a child.

Sea fishing had been introduced to her life recently and since September all of her family went down to the beach instead of just Dad and Grandad. Every few weeks they would go and set up a fire started with pine cones and small sticks as they fished the sea. Each visit they gathered a few bags of driftwood for the next time and dried it out so the fire wouldn't be too smoky. The fire on the beach was enough to keep them warm, these days were always cold. Living by the sea is living with the wind and knowing that the cold is here on or the way at any moment.

Everything went to plan as Laura and her family lived their magical December. As tradition had it, on Christmas eve she woke up and put on her red dress. This year it was decorated with patterns of tiny Santa boots, she brushed her hair and walked down the stairs. She paused near the bottom to hear someone or something, she felt that feeling again, the feeling of a magical presence.

"Hello." she whispered. Laura waited a little longer. Then called a little louder "Hello."

She jumped up into the air as he walked into view and exploded with a "Ho Ho Ho. I do believe you have been expecting me." through his big grin.

Laura stayed still, looking up at the magical man. "Santa." she whispered and then she looked down at his boot. "It was all true! I never even questioned it. I just took it as one of my many dreams. It is not easy to hold on to something you cannot see or feel."

Santa smiled "It was true Laura, come down stairs and let me spend the day with you, I am happy to say I have already been greeted by your grandmother. I hope you will both allow me to be with your family today and show me some of your ways."

Grandma put out her arms for Laura to run into. "Thank you my dear." She cried a little cry and smiled an everlasting smile.

In the kitchen breakfast was being cooked and Santa helped with the cookies. He laughed his "Ho Ho Ho" non-stop, filled with happiness sharing the joys of Christmas Eve in a way he had never done before. He was big, bright and colourful just as we all hear about. A giant with the joys of life.

The craft session was special and he invited Winston to help make a few extra decorations. They sat around the table together with music playing in the background. Roy Wood was singing about how he wished it could be Christmas every day.

"Winston is the greatest toy maker back home and he has won the best decoration competition more times than any elf." bellowed Santa. He was not good at being quiet, he was always loud and this is why on the Eve of Christmas he usually said nothing apart from occasionally slipping out his very well known "Ho Ho Ho".

Winston was glad to hear the praise Santa shared with the family and he proudly handed them each a decoration. Three Snowmen, an Elf and a Santa all made of driftwood, they were all perfect carvings.

"What now" Penny asked, "fishing? Or a little dance?"

"Slade played as Santa danced around the kitchen with Penny. Noddy Holder filled the room with his magic. Santa loved to hear him sing so much that he did not attempt to sing along, even in the chorus.

Grandad went up ahead with Dad and set up a beach fire so when the others arrived, they had a central point, a place to be and to be a little warmer.

Winston was very excited to fish. He was first there, over the years Grandad and Dad had bought one or two too many fishing rods but it turned out today that too many was just enough.

Winston watched as Dad cast the worm and sinker far out to sea. He had never fished so he had never cast before. He was all focused as he was shown what to do and what not to do to make things work. He put the sinker and scary looking hook behind him and he flicked with all of his might, remembering it was all about timing and he released at the right moment. He waited to see how far the sinker would go and it plopped not too far away, nowhere near where he was waiting for it to land.

"Is that ok?" Winston jumped up and down, eyes wide as he looked around like he waited for an applause.

"That is the perfect start for the first time." said Dad, smiling and nodding.

They all stood in a line for a few minutes before the rods were left on the rod rests and they all went to the fire.

"What do we do, what do we do now?" shouted Winston jumping up and down.

"We wait." replied Dad.

Marshmallows were soon being roasted on the very open fire. Chestnuts were wrapped in foil, hot sausages and turkey sandwiches with stuffing were being enjoyed.

Warm comfort foods are a must when fishing and at Christmas time.

Santa took a walk down the beach with only Penny. She talked to him about her wish and her dream of making life better for people.

"You were such a special child. It is the ones that grow up into special adults that make this all worthwhile. I like to give everyone a chance but all I can do is give you what you need. The simplest of things can go a long way. A whistle can make you feel heard and safe, a boat can give you a sense of adventure, a cricket bat, a baseball bat, a football. When a child asks for one of these things, they already know what they would like to be, they are already on the way."

"I never wanted anything". Penny said "I just loved whatever I got, it was being surrounded by everyone and their happiness that I always enjoyed."

"You wanted everything, Penny. And you got it, you made it happen even when you were a child. You held it all together and this is not an easy thing to do."

"Thank you." she whispered and Santa took her into his arms.

"You will make a fine Elf, Penny."

Back at the fire they all reeled in and they each had a fish. It was enough to make Winston sing and dance even more. He was like a kid at Christmas.

"Can I do this again?" he asked.

"You can do this whenever you like. I am sure you can adjust time enough to give yourself a few hours of fishing." Santa answered. "It is nice to see you so relaxed. You are always way too busy.

"I think I should have a fishing rod for Christmas." Winston looked up at Santa, smiled and winked.

Santa laughed his laugh and they all cast out for one more. Waiting can be fun if you know how to wait.

The sea looked and sounded rough but everything felt calm. This felt to them all like the best place to be right now.

"I need to be gone soon. Back to what I do and who I am." Santa smiled as they reeled in another fish. "I have had a lovely time with you all. Fishing on the beach on Christmas Eve has got to be one of the most magical things I have ever done. Spending time with you all has filled me with so much happiness, and, we all know what Winston thought of it! You will have him again next year when he takes some time off. I always think that I am filled right to the brim with the magic in life and then a little more is added. Thank you all."

"One more song." said Grandma and she started to sing. "You better watch out, You better not cry, you better be good I'm telling you why." They all joined in with the chorus.

"Santa Claus is coming to town."

The song got faster and was longer than usual, just so the moment could last a little longer.

Santa moved in close to Penny and looked right into her eyes. "Thank you for my wish. Thank you for everything you have done for so many people. I have wanted to meet you for many years. Next time I will just come and visit, there will be no need for a wish." he smiled again, stared deep into her eyes and held her gaze. It was like he was sharing a secret with her and only she could know. The secret was not spoken, just shared.

"The boot, it was no mistake?" Laura cried out; tears of joy filled her happy eyes.

"Do you really think Santa would make a mistake with so much responsibility, magic and dear old Winston at my side?"

Penny held tightly onto the hand Laura had reached out for her and they said "Happy Christmas" to Santa and Winston for the last time this year. Before they walked away Santa looked at Penny one more time. "Wait here, stay with your family for now."

He turned and walked away with Winston, up into the sand dunes and out of sight.

The family saw the sleigh arrive from the sky; within seconds it was over but it would last forever. As they all huddled close around the fire, they laughed out loud to the bellowing sound of "Ho Ho Ho" over the sea.

THE END

ABOUT THE AUTHOR

Derek Allan is from Northumberland in the United Kingdom.

He loves people, words thoughts and life.

His has a gift with words and uses this gift in many ways.

As a teenager he wrote a children's book called "Magic Gloves" and then at 17 documented his love of cricket in "A diary of a Cricket Season"

Over time he has written many novels, countless poems and short stories. It is something that has always happened, no matter what other projects he takes part in.

Derek has spent most of his time as a full-time musician. Writing beautiful lyrics to songs that have been part of taking him across the UK, Europe and America.

He is also a massive charity supporter and has raised thousands of pounds for many different causes. Organising fundraisers. mostly walks, see his book titled "Footprints for others". This is also name of his charity.